D1399583

DISCARDED

For Hassan,
a happy camper

Library of Congress Cataloging-in-Publication Data.   Cummings, Pat.   Petey Moroni's Camp Runamok diary / by Pat Cummings. — 1st ed.      p.      cm.      Summary: It takes a while for the campers to figure out what is happening to all their food that keeps disappearing. ISBN 0-02-725513-1 [1. Camps—Fiction. 2. Raccoons—Fiction.] I. Title. PZ7.C9148Pe 1992      [E]—dc20      91-45774

# PETEY MORONI'S

CAMP RUNAMOK

# DIARY

## by Pat Cummings

BRADBURY PRESS    NEW YORK

Maxwell Macmillan Canada    Toronto

Maxwell Macmillan International

New York    Oxford    Singapore    Sydney

**DAY 1**

Louie laid his hot dog down for two minutes while he went through his entire suitcase looking for Issue #14 of *Samurai Surfer*. It was a great issue, because Samurai Surfer meets Bonzai Dave for only the second time, and this time on Earth.

Anyway, Louie turned around and his hot dog was *gone*. Not just plain gone or dropped down a crack behind the bunk, but disappeared!

**DAY 2**

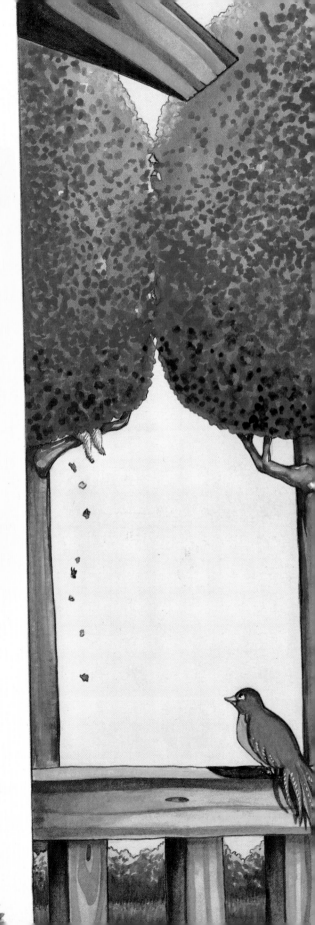

Nancy Patanky *knew*
she had three boxes of
individually wrapped fruit-
flavored Puff n' Stuff
Pastries she brought from
home, but two whole boxes
were missing.

And she really looked.

**DAY 3**

Todd Putter and Dwight Lipsky both said they saw a huge, fat, furry, masked monster with sharp claws running off with a bag of Cheezy Twists when they were in the kitchen refilling their squirt guns.

Louie said, "They're only six years old."
So nobody believed them.

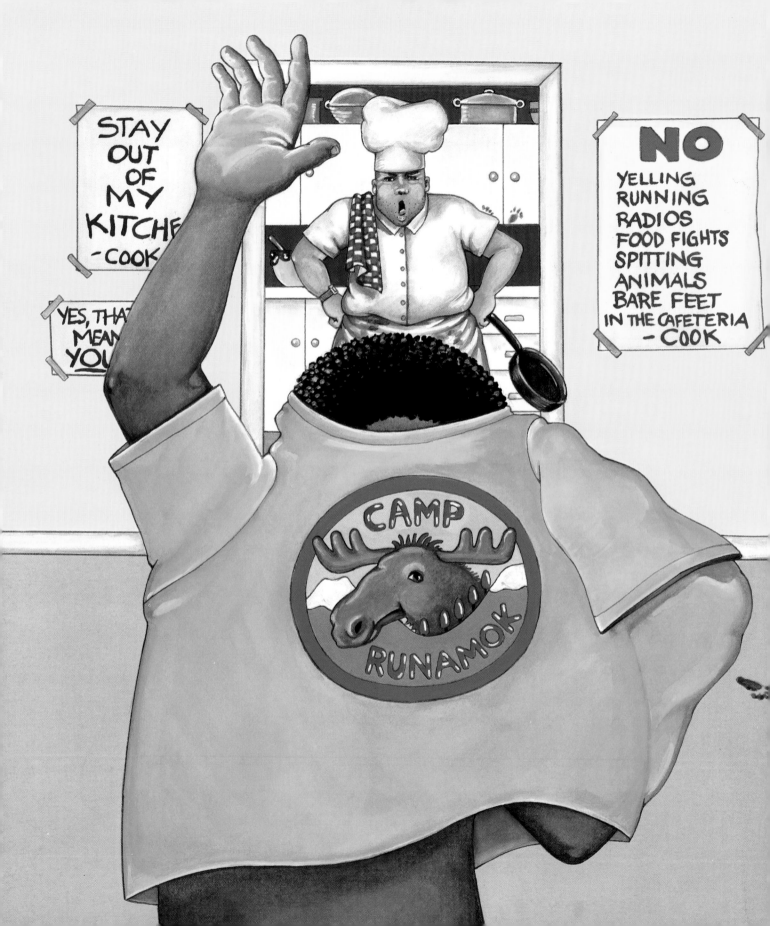

**DAY**

**4**

We got our Camp Runamok T-shirts. That was good, but a whole bowl of brownie mix got licked clean, so there went dessert. Cook suspected Ollie and Nelson. But there were little chocolate footprints all over the kitchen. They weren't Nelson's. They sure weren't big-foot Ollie's, either.

The art teacher with the stiff hair said it was just raccoons.

Louie says Samurai Surfer would catch this thing, no matter how big it was or how many sharp teeth it had.

"Hide the food," was all Ruthie Potts said.

Louie tied a hot dog on a string and sat up almost all night with it hanging out the window, like he was fishing or something.

**DAY 6**

Ollie saw Louie's string hanging out the window on his way to bury his entire supply of Caramel Crunchies. The ones *without* nuts, in the purple bag.

**DAY 7**

Camp meeting was really loud.

Theo, the lifeguard, said the raccoons would leave us alone if we left them alone.

"They got my root-beer Gummy Worms," shouted Millie.

"Try carrots," said Theo.

"I'm missing three bags of marshmallows," said Todd.

"Gripe, gripe, gripe," said Theo.

Everyone from Cabin 4 yelled, "Hide the food! Lock the refrigerator! Let's eat everything!"

**DAY 8**

Barney O'Connell's box from home was empty and all chewed on. The Raisin Dots and every single double-stuffed Choco-Log were gone.

This means war.

**DAY**

**9**

Barney was the leader and we found a hole in the woods. Nobody would poke too far. Louie told us to put some candy in front of the hole. But not his. Everybody is running out of stuff, anyway.

Then Millie fell in a bush and we stopped.

**DAY 10**

It got all of Ruthie Potts' Great Grape Bubble Gobs. And Ollie found nothing but a hole where he put his Caramel Crunchies. We're having a meeting tomorrow, except for Millie. She's got poison ivy.

Girls.

**DAY 11**

So we all go to Cabin 4 and listen to Louie and Ollie fighting over who's boss. Then Dwight says, "Make a trap like the one Tackhead was caught in by the Metaloids."

Ruthie said, "Let's just eat all our stuff NOW!"

Nelson said, "Let's hang everything up."

So we did.

**DAY**

**12**

Louie said this reminded him of the time Bonzai Dave had to hide the speckled space pods, and they were right over Samurai Surfer's head for three whole pages. Ruthie wanted her Lemon Dots back to eat right away. Todd said nobody could get to our stuff now. Nobody and nothing.

It didn't work.

**DAY**

**14**

We had to leave today. We never got our stuff back. Big-foot Ollie got on the bus with a whole bag of Chocolate Chewies he had hidden all the time in his socks. They were pretty soft and had a little sock fuzz on them. But they didn't taste bad....

Next summer we'll get that raccoon for sure.